Sadie, Ori, and Nuggles Go to Camp

To Conundrum and his fuzzy friends —J.K.
For Don, with love—J.F.

KAR-BEN PUBLISHING
A division of Lerner Publishing Group, Inc.
241 First Avenue North
Minneapolis, MN 55401 USA
1-800-4-KARBEN

Website address: www.karben.com

Library of Congress Cataloging-in-Publication Data

Korngold, Jamie S.
    Sadie, Ori, and Nuggles go to camp / by Jamie Korngold ; illustrated by
Julie Fortenberry.
        pages   cm
    Summary: When older sister Sadie and her first-time camper brother Ori
prepare to spend the summer at Jewish sleep-away camp, Ori wonders if
he should bring his beloved stuffed animal Nuggles.
    ISBN 978-1-4677-0424-3 (lib. bdg. : alk. paper)
    [1. Camps—Fiction. 2. Fear—Fiction. 3. Toys—Fiction. 4. Jews—United States—
Fiction.] I. Fortenberry, Julie, 1956- illustrator. II. Title.
    PZ7.K83749Sag 2014
    [E]—dc23   2013021753

PJ Library Edition ISBN 978-1-4677-8592-1

Manufactured in China
3-46962-19403-10/18/2022

0623/B0662/A4

Sadie, Ori, and Nuggles Go to Camp

By Jamie Korngold

illustrated by Julie Fortenberry

KAR-BEN
PUBLISHING

Sadie loved camp.

She loved performing in the camp play,

and playing basketball.

She loved singing songs around the campfire,

and swimming in the lake.

She loved whispering with her friends late at night,

and Ice Cream Sundaes Day.

Best of all, she loved the friends she made at camp.

Camp was the only place in Sadie's life where everyone was Jewish.

During the school year, she was the only Jewish kid in her class. But at camp, she didn't have to explain.

And this year her brother Ori had turned seven, finally old enough to come with her. They were both so excited!

Sadie helped Ori get ready for camp.

"Are you going to bring Nuggles?" Sadie asked,
while they were packing his duffel bag.

Nuggles was his favorite stuffy. Ori had slept with Nuggles every single night since he was born.

"I can't fall asleep without Nuggles, and he will miss me if I leave him home," Ori said, "but if I bring him, all the other kids will make fun of me."

"It's okay to bring him," Sadie said.

"But then the kids will think
I'm a baby," said Ori.

Ori didn't know what to do. "Why don't you try sleeping without Nuggles tonight and see how it goes," Ori's mother suggested. "We can put him in the duffel bag in the morning if you decide you want to bring him."

Ori put Nuggles on the shelf. After his mom and dad kissed him good-night and turned off the light, he tried to snuggle his pillow instead, but it just wasn't the same.

He tried to count sheep to distract himself,
but he just got bored.

He tossed and turned, and turned and tossed, and tossed and turned some more, until finally he got out of bed and took Nuggles off the shelf.

Ori snuggled close to Nuggles and fell quickly asleep.

In the morning
he put Nuggles in his duffel.

After breakfast, Sadie and Ori's parents helped them pile their bags in the trunk.

As they drove to camp,
Sadie talked excitedly about
seeing her friends again.

Ori worried. Would he like the kids
in his cabin? Would he get a top bunk?
Would he fall off the top bunk?

Would the other kids like soccer as much as he did? But most of all, he worried that the kids would make fun of him for sleeping with Nuggles.

He had waited for months to go to camp, but now he wasn't so sure.

Before he knew it, they arrived.

"Shalom," said a friendly young man as Ori got out of the car. "I'm Jonah and I will be your counselor. Let's put your stuff in the cabin, and you can meet your new friends. We're about to play soccer."

Ori didn't say a word as he followed Jonah into the cabin.

Ori looked around. Each of the boys in his cabin was sitting on a bunk bed. And on each bunk bed he saw a well-loved stuffy.

There were lions, bears, tigers, and even a zebra who was missing an eye.

"I'm going to like camp," Ori said.
And he did!